The Little Yellow Digger
Goes to School

Betty & Alan Gilderdale

SCHOLASTIC

AUCKLAND SYDNEY NEW YORK LONDON TORONTO
MEXICO CITY NEW DELHI HONG KONG

D1294974

The little yellow digger
was coming to our school.
The principal had asked it
to dig a swimming pool.

It clattered through the playground.
It came at morning tea.
The driver smiled, "Good morning!"
as we ran around to see.

The bell was ringing loudly.
We had to go to class.
The digger chugged across the field
to dig beneath the grass.

7

We crowded round the windows
to see what we could see,
as it began to make a hole
where the pool would be.

9

Our principal went out to look
(his name was Mr Lane) …

but then the digger hit a pipe
and burst the water main!

A fountain spurted upwards.
It was a water spout!
Then it cascaded downwards …
the driver yelled, "Look out!"

Poor Mr Lane was knocked down flat,
and soaking wet, right through.
"Look what you've done!" he shouted.
"Whatever can we do?"

The water went on gushing
with a swooshing, swishing sound.
It quickly made great puddles
on the muddy football ground.

Just then another teacher
rushed out to lend a hand.
He slipped and slithered on the mud.
He couldn't even stand!

The office phoned the Council:
"Come quickly as you can!"

It wasn't very long before
they sent a helpful man.

He stopped the gushing fountain
once the hydrant had been found,
but said there'd be no water
in the buildings all around.

19

"The bathrooms will be out of use,"
said worried Mr Lane.

"I know! We'll picnic on the beach until they've fixed the main."

Just then the Council truck arrived,
the men unpacked their load,
but we'd fetched hats and lunches
and were marching down the road.

22

Then, while we picnicked on the beach,
the digger worked again
to help the council workmen
repair the broken main.

When we returned at three o'clock,
the water was back on.

The digger was still working.
The men and truck had gone.

Now, every time we have a swim
in our new swimming pool,
we remember how the digger
had visited our school ...

the unexpected picnic ...

a muddy Mr Lane ...

we do so hope the digger
will come to school again!

Acknowledgements

We would like to acknowledge with gratitude the help and advice received from Ray Richards and Nicky Wallace of Richards Literary Agency during the writing and illustration of this book.

We would particularly like to thank Holly Cutfield, who posed so patiently, and Alistair Wallace, who not only posed for his picture but lent us his soccer ball!